What Goes Up...

A Science Fiction Short Story

Ed Teja

Float Street Press

Things grow popular, then fall into obscurity. We embrace isolationism and then globalism and back again. We favor complete independence and then swing to crying for government protections. We want communication and then rail because we want to disconnect and get alone time.

And so we see the rise and fall of nearly every-thing.

Contents

WHAT GOES UP...

Whenever Oswald Cropper went into Granny Grace's home office, the first thing he noticed was the slightly antiseptic smell. It was the same smell he noticed when she took him to her office at the lab. In fact, her home office was, in every important way, exactly like Granny Grace's office at the lab.

Both spaces were tidy, well-lighted, and spotlessly clean. The table surfaces were smooth ("non-porous," she told him) and nothing but the sign over her desk was anything but functional.

Granny Grace's offices were hardly comfortable places — they were, to use Granny Grace's favorite and highest complimentary term, efficient.

Oswald enjoyed being around Granny Grace. Happily, when he turned ten, his parents allowed him to spend a summer working under her super-vision as an intern in her lab.

It was great fun. He met exciting people, did simple chores that let the important people focus on their work, and had his very own access badge to a lab that most people didn't even know existed.

Even his own parents weren't allowed in those hallowed, if spartan, halls.

Granny Grace liked rules so much that she not only enforced the lab rules (strictly, rigidly) but had extra rules just for her office. Oswald was expected to know and obey them, the big and small, equally.

Whenever she felt the need to remind him of one (or more) of those rules, she would put on a stern look and explain, in almost exactly the same words, whatever it was he had neglected, forgotten, or ignored.

Oswald always felt bad when he broke the rules. For a moment or two, he'd want nothing more than to go home. And yet... her lab and her entire world were filled with exciting things. Granny always had an interesting experiment going on, some empirical study that involved monitoring myriad dials and gauges, flashing LEDs, and computer readouts. Once she'd used an alarm that was so shrill, so loud, when it went off it made his ears ache for minutes after it stopped.

He even liked the sign... the one hanging over her desk, the only sign that didn't say something like

"Caution" or "Oxygen in Use" or "Emergency Use Only."

The words on the sign were the same ones you saw everywhere, of course, but this sign was special. Granny Grace had paid someone to engrave them in a shiny, metal plaque that was mounted on genuine synthetic wood. The metal was brass, although the first time he saw it, wanting to show he was impressed, Oswald made a mistake — an observational error, it was called. "That's a nice bronze plaque," he said.

That earned him a scowl. "Now, now... don't rush to judgment without facts."

"It's not bronze?"

"No," she said, speaking calmly and carefully. "Bronze is an alloy of copper and tin. This is brass... an alloy of copper and zinc. Things being similar doesn't make them the same and calling it bronze based on appearance, especially from such a distance... that is not a scientific way to approach the world around you. That is a bad habit that violates the very principle the sign expresses."

Oswald had always thought that, if middle names reflected a person's character (and he thought they should), then Granny Grace would have been Granny Precision Grace.

The sign over the desk, the one in question, the one with the words engraved in brass, not bronze, said:

"The LAW demands scientific thinking because SCIENCE shows us the truth."

Yup, it was written just like that, as it always was wherever he saw it, even though Oswald's English teacher had explained that the capitalization of the words LAW and SCIENCE was incorrect, that it was an over-the-top usage that was intended to add unneeded emphasis.

Granny Grace, however, wasn't impressed to hear that. She wasn't concerned about language skills beyond those required to "present experimental data and analysis in a clear and concise manner."

That's what she told him, rather severely, when he pointed out what he saw as a mistake.

Her willingness to grant latitude for imprecision in slogans confused him. "It is imprecise," he said.

"Violating an arbitrary convention concerning typography does NOT," she said, capitalizing the word with her voice, "make something imprecise. In fact, the very violation calls attention to the special meaning we give those words."

Hearing her tone of voice, certain she would allow no room for discussion, and showing wisdom beyond his meager (although rich) ten years, Oswald let her have the last word. Winning a debate with Granny Grace was hard, nearly impossible for a stalwart, well-informed, opinionated, and thick-skinned (perhaps with the thickness of a rhino or elephant skin) adult, much less a ten-year-old grandchild.

Like most people in those days, Granny Grace only felt comfortable only when the balance of society's values had tipped heavily in favor of science. People were fickle, and the balance of power, of ascendancy, was a delicate thing.

"Like weights on a mechanical balance," she said. "What goes up can always come down. It doesn't take much. The public acts on appearances."

Knowing that she worked hard to maintain the status quo, even to the point of saying that the witch trials had been an unfortunate historical necessity. "It needs to be kept simple for the public," she told Oswald.

In other words, Science, good. Magic, bad.

Oswald's Granny Grace wasn't just a true believer; no, she was a Scientist. Not many people could say that. In fact, out of the entire billions of people on the planet, despite there being millions of people working in scientific fields, only one thousand five hundred carefully screened, thoroughly vetted people in the world were allowed to call themselves Scientists. They were the ones who had proven themselves to be disciples of true Science. (And yes, with a capital "S" to emphasize it.)

Once a person was designated a Scientist, they became part of the elite, the lawmakers. Each Scientist had a spot on the International Science Council Triumvirate, which comprised three groups, each consisting of five hundred Scientists. These stalwarts rotated responsibilities (changing every quarter) for vetting new scientific breakthroughs and principles. They adjudicated what was good science, what was valid, repeatable, and empirically determined, and what was not (commonly referred to, depending on the speaker, as either fake science, wrong thinking, or drivel.)

In history classes at school, Oswald had learned that there had been a time when laws had been based on something vague and indeterminate called politics.

While he could never find a clear and succinct definition of the term, leastwise, one that made any sense, he knew there had once been a group called a Supreme Court. This group was sort of like the Triumvirate, but they determined the course of public life based on strange concepts called precedence and case law. There wasn't one pragmatic scientific principle involved at any level.

Of course, once people learned the true value of Science and realized that laws needed a scientific basis if there would be any hope of establishing a fair, clear, and consistent vision, they replaced the appointed judges, who knew nothing about Science, with Scientists. That gave public life Science-based rules that provided explicit standards and methodologies for understanding the world.

And so a hierarchical division grew up between Scientists and those who worked in science.

Oswald's mother, Granny Grace's daughter, was a board-certified biochemist and ran the entire biochemistry department at Phial Industries. Although her license allowed her to practice science (with a lower-case "s") legitimately, she was NOT a Scientist.

She could not practice law.

Much to Granny Grace's chagrin, Oswald's father was a businessman who ran a freight company. As a businessman, he used scientific principles, of course, but did not innovate. A small company like his couldn't afford the Scientist it would be legally required to hire to engage in any sort of thinking outside of the norms. And business science was deemed relatively unimportant, so his father stuck to the tried-and-true ways of doing business.

Oswald was too young to understand, but of course, we all know that no matter how efficient, fair, equitable, and just a system might be, regardless of how many gushing platitudes are applied to it, there will be those who do not benefit from it as much as others.

Those people, malcontents, according to Granny Grace, raised arguments the law of Science was not particularly benign, that it had a darker side. Only allowing Scientists to innovate, it had been suggested, even was in opposition to evolution.

In short, not everyone liked it. Granny Grace was of the fierce opinion that these arguments arose, not from logic, but due to defects in their cognitive abilities. Her (esteemed) view was that people who think Science is not always true or balanced, are not good citizens. Disgruntled and sour people, she called them. Often, when discussing the malcontents, the word 'barbarians' came up in her analysis.

Whenever she said something like that, Oswald knew she was thinking of his Granny Jill — Oswald's father's mother.

Oswald liked Granny Jill every bit as much as he did Granny Grace. She was the accountant for his father's freight company and, when he was about ten, she was living with them.

One night when his parents had invited Granny Jill to dinner, the conversation turned to careers — various avenues Oswald might want to think about and begin to direct his studies toward (he had excellent aptitude scores for every scientific field). He had looked at Granny Jill and asked: "You are really smart. Why don't you work in a science job?"

The question embarrassed his parents, especially his mother, but Granny Jill let out a big laugh and beamed her wonderful, high-wattage smile at him. Granny Jill smiled a lot.

"I used to work in science," she said. "Until they caught me at it."

Oswald had never heard of anyone stopping work before, much less losing their career. After all, career paths were set by the Science Council and you applied to work in them, with the results being based on grades, references from teachers, and internship colleagues.

You needed to show that your efforts would be efficient and effective, and useful to society.

"What happened?" he asked. "What do you mean, they caught you?"

"Things go up and then they come down. My degrees are in parapsychology," she said.

"Fake science," his mother said.

Granny Jill ignored her. "I was happily making inroads, conducting perfectly legal, ethically sound experiments on telekinesis and ESP when the council decided, one bright summer morning, with no warning or discussion, that anything with 'para' in it, such as paranormal, was no longer science. Perhaps they thought it should be lumped in with studies of parachuting. At any rate, I was told that my studies, along with any empirical research into the supernatural or any aspect of the unseen realms of the mind and spirit, were henceforth banned." She laughed. "They really used the damn word 'henceforth,' in the declaration."

Then she leaned across the table and whispered loudly. "Truth is, the silly bastards were scared of what I'd find. They realized there were some rocks they didn't want people to look under."

"Mother!" Oswald's mother said.

Then his mother dug out a very serious, seriously adult face, her most serious, from somewhere and put it on. He never thought she looked that good in it.

"Oswald," she said, "the committee determined that, due to years of effort providing any empirical evidence that those things even existed, their study was deemed to be not pragmatic. They are, after all, no more than a variant of witchcraft."

"Horse hockey," Granny Jill said.

"Your Granny Jill didn't agree with the ruling. Instead of appealing and following procedure, she continued her research."

Granny Jill chuckled. "It sure pissed off your mom when I got arrested."

After her trial, Daddy hired Granny Jill as his accountant. That job was deemed a trade and only required that she join the guild and take a test on bookkeeping, which she passed almost too easily for Granny Grace's taste.

"She needs something to do and that job will force her to apply scientific principles to her work," his father pointed out. "There is nothing in the least paranormal about accounting."

I think Oswald knew better, even then, that his father always had a weakness for the whimsical and strange. He tried not to show it, as one does any unsociable traits, but everyone saw it. Granny Grace claimed he inherited it from his mother. "An intensive, regressive genetic scan should reveal what his problem is," she told Mommy more than once.

But after several years of quietly keeping the accounts and demonstrating a strange and unexpected affinity for finance that made the family rather wealthy, even Granny Grace accepted her in her role.

Not that Granny Grace started trusting Granny Jill, and she certainly didn't like her, but she did acknowledge that her uncanny ability to buy stocks before they went up in price was useful.

"She must be applying scientific principles more rigorously than most people do," she said. Grudging but heartfelt praise, indeed.

That summer, Oswald's father decided he should work with Granny Jill. "It will be good for him to taste business before you and your mother totally immerse him in science," he said. "Balance is Science, after all."

Oswald's mother didn't like the idea, but in the interest of fairness, she agreed. After all, he had spent the previous summer interning in Granny Grace's lab. Oswald's father didn't really think that much of Science, but had felt it would be good for the boy and now he was only asking they broaden his education. Sooner or later, he'd be thinking about careers. "He can't do that without experience," he said. So she allowed it.

And what a delightful contrast that summer turned out to be. Granny Jill did her work in a hopelessly cluttered office that smelled of sage and cinnamon; classical music played softly in the background. There were no pages. She would get up anytime she wanted and make tea, and they would have a cookie or two.

She taught Oswald the basics of double-entry bookkeeping and he found he had an aptitude for it. There was a delicious joy in adding things up and cross-referencing the numbers to check that everything balances. All the fascination he found in Granny Grace's empirical experiments was there, and here, with Granny Jill, it was coupled with sheer joy. A love of life.

Granny Jill would open the windows (the lab had no windows) to let in the fresh air. She would laugh at nothing, chat with the birds that landed on the sill (she put cookie crumbs on it to attract them) and seemed pleased with the world in general.

And she wasn't even working in science. It was amazing.

Another difference in their work and workplaces was the concept of order. Working as an intern for Granny Grace, he was expected to have a place for everything and ensure that everything wound up back in its rightful place. "Otherwise, you'll never know where anything is," she said. "That is the logic of Science. Order is important."

The chaos and clutter of Granny Jill's world, while making it homey, made such organization difficult, and yet, she never seemed to find it necessary. Although she didn't have "places for things" where he was expected to return them, he realized that he had never heard Granny Jill spend a single moment asking herself: "Now where did I put that?"

If she needed a pen to jot down a note, if she had to grab her reading glasses to check a figure, or locate the mouse to open a spreadsheet, if she needed anything at all, it always seemed to be right where she needed it when she needed it.

"How do you find things?" he asked.

"If you have a good relationship with your tools, if you trust them, you don't ever need to find them," she said.

"You don't?"

She winked. "Not if you treat them well. After all, they know as well as you do when they are needed. It's easier if they find you. And more convenient for them, I might add."

"But how would they know?"

"The right working of things," she said.

"Is that a scientific principle?"

She grinned. "Not anymore, I'm afraid. It used to be, and it works so well, too."

She pointed to a stack of invoices. Over the week, she'd piled them up as they came in. "What is the rule for entering invoices?" she asked him.

"You have to organize them by date and do the oldest ones first," he said, proud to have remembered.

"But if you get behind..." she laughed, "the way I've let them pile up, my... that would be a big job. Fortunately, on this desk, the most important things rise to the top."

"All by themselves?"

She looked around. "Must be. I don't see anyone else. But then, I've never asked that question. If that kind of research was legal, we could run some experiments and find out. Granny Grace would roll over in her grave."

"But she isn't dead," Oswald said.

"I try not to think of that," Granny Jill said.

"I don't think a stack of papers will sort itself. I think you are teasing me."

She nodded. "A reasonable thing to think. I am a bit of a tease. So we need to find out." She pointed at a desk. "We've had invoices come in every day this week, so if this was a regular desk, most of the ones we need to enter first would be on the bottom. But if I'm telling the truth, you'll find them smack dab on top."

Oswald liked the way she talked, using words no one else did, like "smack dab." Those words, not being scientific, drove his mother crazy, but his father always seemed to know exactly what she meant.

He went to the stack and picked up invoices from the top. It was a rather large stack, but sure enough, the ones on top were not the most recent. In fact, he remembered the top one. It had come in on Monday. Curious, he stuck his hand under the stack and pulled one from the bottom. It was one he'd printed out himself (it had been emailed to them) that very day. And he clearly remembered Granny Jill telling him to just toss it on the stack.

"You snuck in and sorted them," he said to her.

"When did I do that?" she asked. "Those are all miscellaneous expenses. I hadn't even thought about them until we started talking about them a few minutes ago."

Still convinced it was a trick, Oswald said no more. And he certainly wasn't going to say anything to his parents. Working with Granny Jill was too much fun, and if his mother thought she was playing tricks on him or trying to make him think something unscientific was going on, well, she had no sense of humor anymore and might not let him go back. Daddy would just grin, but once his mother put her foot down, well, that would be the end of the discussion.

One day, after he'd quite gotten the hang of doing the ledgers and preparing the weekly figures (so his father could see if business was up or down, if expenses were under control), Oswald had the experience no accountant ever wants to have. He found that the books didn't balance.

He hated telling Granny Jill, but he forced himself to blurt it out. She lit a candle, even though it wasn't dark or anything, and passed a hand over the flame. "Tell me, Oswald, is the error divisible by nine?" she asked.

It was. "Yes. Is that good?"

"Neither good nor bad. It simply means that you transposed two numbers," she said.

He remembered what that meant. "Like I wrote 87 when I should have written 78."

"Exactly. See how we used a simple, harmless trick to point us toward the right answer?"

He did, but... "But that isn't a solution. How do we find the actual error?" he asked.

She bent over him and he smelled her lavender perfume as she pointed to the columns of figures. "We have two choices," she said. "The way most people like to do it, the way Scientists want us to do it, is to check every entry, one after the other. If you don't make the same mistake, comparing all of your entries to the original invoices will do it."

"That will take a long time," he said. His heart sank. That looked like a lot of work. There were a lot of numbers to check.

"It is. A lot of science is dull and boring. They didn't like my studies in part because they didn't understand them, and partly because my work can involve some of the same repetition their research does. Repeatability demonstrates that something, a phenomenon, is real and controllable. But if we ignore the scientific protocols, then we are free to fix the problem using The Nudge."

"The Nudge?"

She grinned. "Do you think it matters that we determine which figure you transposed?"

"Sure. Then I can fix it."

"What if you could get it to fix itself?"

"What?"

"You found the error. The figure knows it is wrong and was waiting for us to notice. So what if we could simply nudge it and get it to fix itself?"

"That would be cool."

"Wouldn't it?" She ran a finger down the column and hummed a soft little tune that he didn't recognize. Suddenly, something on the page changed, something was different, but Oswald wasn't sure what. "All fixed," she said cheerfully.

"What changed?" he asked. He looked at the totals and suddenly, they matched.

"I have no idea at all," Granny Jill said. "The incorrect number is now correct."

"But you changed something."

"You saw what I did. I touched some figures that were incorrect and simply nudged them in the right direction. I hummed something soft and reassuring, then ran my finger down the columns to coax everything to align correctly.

With that encouragement, they put themselves right. You might have heard a little click when it happened, a minor twinkle in the optic field. That was the universe snapping things back into alignment, putting them the way they are supposed to be."

Over the next days, he saw her do it with a lot of things that "weren't quite right." Each time, she used the Nudge, to make them the way they should be.

"Whenever you nudge things, that sure seems a lot like magic to me," he complained one day.

"Is it?" she asked, smiling broadly. "I call it applying the scientific principle of the right working of things. Nature prefers things to be correct."

"It sure isn't Science," the ten-year-old insisted.

"Well, to be clear, I don't really do anything at all... I just point out that they are out of alignment — I manifest a Nudge. Actually, people do it all the time, even your Granny Grace."

"She wouldn't alter results," Oswald said firmly, demonstrating loyalty.

"No, and neither do I. When I suggest they get right, they do it themselves. Haven't you watched Granny Grace's face when she is running experiments and watching the data arrive in real time?"

Oswald laughed. "She makes great faces, like scowling will make the data behave."

"If she knew how to do it correctly, how to manifest a Nudge, then it would. This way, she has erratic results. If she were willing to let people like me research it properly, then she could apply it with scientific precision. As it is, only a few of us know the proper steps to make what should happen, happen." She held out her hands. "I can teach you the Nudge, if you like, but you can't tell anyone — not because it is bad or wrong, but because it is something they won't understand and therefore fear."

"You might get caught doing that," he said. And she might be punished. Losing Granny Jill would be horrid. After all, she was, and always would be, on probation for studying such things. Science mandated that repeat offenders were always severely punished.

"Maybe, but that seems unlikely unless you tell someone. We don't need to hide its use as long as we don't talk about it. As you've seen, the Science Council auditors check our books every single month. They ensure that we are following authorized scientific accounting principles. All this time and they have never had a single complaint about our accounting methods and believe me, they look for something to not like. That's what auditors do. And they know my record, so every month they look hard before they certify that our bookkeeping complies with all scientific principles." She smiled. "The way I understand the law, that means my methods must be scientific."

Then she winked. "At least it seems that way to me. But then, I'm not a Scientist."

And so Oswald learned the Nudge. It was as simple as Granny Jill had said and fun, too. He saw himself tickling things into proper alignment, and what harm ever came from making things correct?

After a time, he saw other things in the world that weren't quite correct, things other people had put into place and left that way.

When he asked, Granny Jill taught him how to sense the force holding them in place. Then he could feel its energy. It took a lot more than a tickle to fix them and could be tiring. But as with the Nudge, he didn't actually do anything. It was more like discussing things with the universe and coming to an agreement.

Oswald called the work he did righting big things the Force. Even though he didn't force anything, it required understanding of the forces — and what,

Granny Jill asked, was the process of coming to an understanding of things, but very good science?

Sometimes, according to Granny Jill, the issue wasn't a matter of changing anything at all. Sometimes it was a simple matter of paying attention to existing forces, powers that surrounded us.

For example: "Black tea contains tannin," Granny Jill pointed out. "Tannin has an affinity for certain forces, a tendency to align with specific ones in specific ways that can tell us a lot. This is why gypsies read tea leaves to predict the future."

"Which is foolishness."

"Of course it is," she said. "Unless you know the codes."

"The codes?"

That was when she showed him the patterns the tea could make and how to read them. When she showed him how she had invested the family's money in stocks, using the patterns, and made a fortune, when she explained that the trick was to not get greedy and make a big deal over your success, he saw... well, he saw a pattern there.

Through that summer, Granny Jill showed him that, whatever he was trying to do, he had to think about the way smells and sounds helped or hindered his efforts. Once he noted them, it was up to him to arrange things correctly, put the right bits and pieces together. That meant learning their natures, their qualities.

For some things, like sage, all you had to do was keep them at hand. With no effort on your part at all sage would clear the air and make you feel much better... even when things weren't going well. The strong, acrid smells of disinfectants, on the other hand, made it hard to do anything at all.

Freshness and light, talking to birds, music, she taught, all added to the positive, right working of things, and encouraged the universe to right things that were wrong.

The days passed quickly, and when it was time to go back to school, Oswald found that by using a lot of things that everyone called magic, his grades in science soared. He became a star pupil. He also got Granny Jill to open a brokerage account for him, and he invested some money Granny Grace gave him in some obscure stocks.

Other than that, he was much like any other kid, going to school (but getting all A's now) and alternating his summers, interning (brilliantly) with Granny Grace one year and studying accounting (and the essential extras) with Granny Jill then next.

While he loved both worlds, the hypocrisy of the Scientists, ignoring perfectly natural and useful things, began to annoy him. After all, blending the worlds together was the very thing that made his life good. In his teens, he decided that, in addition to making his mark in science and business, he wanted to change the world. To open everyone's eyes to

The Truth. It was a very idealistic sentiment. A very teenage desire to have. But Oswald was wise (for a teenager) to the world's ways and saw that shouting: "Hey, morons, I've been successful because I use all the tools, including so-called magic," would do nothing but see him ostracized, perhaps locked away. Such an act would not, under any circumstances, be received well.

"Show, don't tell," he'd learned in the same writing class where he'd learned that Granny Grace's sign was typographically, if not grammatically, incorrect.

Granny Jill was not exactly on the same page. When he told her what he had in mind, her actual comment was: "Whatever floats your boat. But don't expect to be loved for telling the world it is wrong."

During his sophomore year at MIT, where Oswald was studying engineering, he decided to take the first step. As his stock was now worth a small fortune, he had all the resources he needed. Tearing apart a cell phone, discarding all the phone circuitry but keeping the camera and processor, he added in some circuits of his own, including a proprietary chip that could perform large Wagnerian expansions in a nanosecond or less, and his own specialized pattern recognition software. He attached a small cup to it, turned it on, and tested it.

When he compared its analysis to his own manual version, the results pleased him.

It worked fine. Then he published a limited challenge online and tweeted it (on social media, not to the birds) and put it everywhere he could think of, making it outrageous and defiant. Instantly (well, within ten minutes) his message was picked up and rebroadcast by Forbes, Fortune, Reuters, Business Week, and every other business press.

The challenge said: "You don't need an extensive education in finance or even a broker to make money in the stock exchange. I've created a digitized stock selection tool I call PersonalStockBrocker that does it for you. I will wager one-hundred-thousand dollars that my device, operated by a person of average intelligence and limited knowledge of markets, can invest five-thousand dollars in the market using my device and outperform any professional broker over a six-month period. The rules are simple: At the end, the one with the most money wins."

There were a lot of details in fine print that no one would ever read, contributed by a lawyer friend of Granny Jill. They added in provisions and provisos, exceptions and exception handling, arbitration, and a ban on arbitrage only because the lawyer didn't know what that meant. They weren't important.

The challenge was largely ignored. Tech was producing strange marvels at a rapid rate. Already the cheap chess program had to spot humans a queen, and most people's cars knew more about where they were than they did. As a result, the fear of losing far outweighed the allure of winning so much money.

Until... There is always a gotcha in the timeline of significant events, and when the president of the Federal Reserve Board mentioned that the device needed to be tested, preferably against humans, so that, if its inventor was onto something, the device could be banned before it fell into "the wrong hands," although he didn't say if he meant terrorists, money launderers, or the Federal Government.

The Federal Reserve, therefore, offered to judge the competition, which brought brokers out of their normal habitat, the woodwork. Especially relevant to their enthusiasm was the line about "the one with the most money wins." Although the statement went without saying in their world, it came across as an endorsement of values, and couldn't be ignored.

The contest was set up and a "typical user" was selected by the Banking Commission. They chose Alexander Murphy, of Tulsa, OK as their ideal candidate. He had no known priors, had never owned stocks (or even a savings account), worked in the custodial department for the city, and was married with two kids, which would ensure heartwarming feature stories.

The Fed Reserve flew Alex, as his friends called him, first-class to Washington, DC because they thought the location would make the event seem more important.

At Alexander's request, his brother-in-law, who was a reporter for a local Tulsa paper, accompanied him to take notes for the inevitable book deal.

At the meeting, the human broker, who had been selected by a jury of his peers, arrived. He wore a three-piece suit and carried a ceremonial Corinthian leather briefcase that contained a single sheet of paper (parchment) listing his chosen investments. He'd written his choice down in private and then had it secretly sealed in an envelope.

Oswald made no advance preparations. He arrived with an electric teapot, water, some tea bags, and the PersonalStockBroker. At his direction, and with the world watching on a live stream, Alex made a nice pot of tea and poured it into a special orifice in the device, then sloshed the tea around before pouring it out through another orifice. Then he pressed a large button that was clearly labeled, "PRESS ME," with the words capitalized out of deference to Granny Grace, who he was sure was watching at home.

The cell phone (remember, this was a cannibalized phone) display helpfully came to life with a stock that no one in the room had ever heard of, to the audible relief of the brokers and bankers present. It was traded on the over-the-counter market, however, and, with no research at all, Oswald turned to the competition's official (head of the New York Stock Exchange) and said: "Place the bet."

"It's an investment," the man said, rather offended.

"Here is my bet," the broker said, handing the envelope over. His stock was an Israeli software company that had seen a recent price decline due to some unfortunate dealings with spy agencies from a host of governments but was widely tipped to soar once the scandals blew over.

No one was to know the names of the stocks either side invested in so that the results would not be influenced.

And with that, the contest began. Alex went back to Tulsa, Oswald went back to studying for his finals at MIT, the brokers and bankers went back in the woodwork, and the business media all put giant countdown clocks for the six months on their websites.

Oswald's tea-leaf reader, of course, won hands down. Alexander came back (with his brother-in-law) for the ceremony and went home happy, having sold his stock for fifty-thousand dollars (three months into the competition, the unknown company announced a verified cure for avian flu); the competing (losing) broker sold his business and retired to the island of St. Vincent, and Oswald gave the hundred thousand dollars he won to a charity that was feeding the homeless in Miami Beach.

"That horrid device is a menace," the entire banking community declared. The government confiscated the prototype and threw it in a river somewhere after making Oswald promise not to make any more or ever explain how it worked.

By that time, he and Granny Jill had completed another project. A book. Capitalizing on his new fame (or notoriety), they co-authored a book called "Potions and spells for a better world."

Given that it had nothing to do with banking, the power elite ignored it. Several prominent Scientists (yes, from the triumvirate) did read it and called, loudly, on podcasts, and social media, for it to be banned. Or burned. Or burned and banned.

"This is garbage, not science," they all said, almost simultaneously.

"This is magic, not science," Granny Jill said when she went on other talk shows and podcasts.

Naturally, the outrage made the book an instant bestseller, and when the publisher got the porn star Stormy Daniels to record the audiobook, that went well too.

Besieged with requests for help in understanding how the spells and potions were manifested and made, Granny Jill launched a video channel where she showed how easily you could learn the Nudge and the Force and apply them to improving your life. Her personality, the delight she took in showing people how to do what they were not supposed to want to do, made the show an enormous hit.

As a result, several authorities invested time investigating their teachings, trying to determine if she and Oswald were doing anything other than happily applying scientific principles (as they claimed they were). They couldn't ever come to a decision.

Meantime, monetizing her channel required the platform's accountants to buy her other book: <u>Accounting Techniques for Unaccountable Things</u>.

For the first time in publishing history, an accounting book hit the bestseller list. Granny Jill was happy to publicly acknowledge that much of its success undoubtedly came from her tendency to play fast and loose with the facts. "I think people are suffering from fact fatigue," she said. "My approach, trusting instincts, comes as a relief."

After years of precision, a lifetime of studying cause and effect, and performing tedious empirical data analysis, the public clamored to know more about hunches, about calculated coincidence, about the magic of things, and how sometimes science was applied magic and sometimes what seemed magical was nothing but applied science.

They blurred together and the pendulum, the dominating force, shifted away from science and toward... well, toward everything vague, inexplicable, magical, light, ethereal, and mostly, anything that made Granny Jill laugh. For she was everyone's Granny Jill now.

Oswald became content. He got his Ph.D. in Physics, won a Nobel Prize for proving the existence of a new subatomic particle that he called the O particle, and then, two years later, he won another one for proving the O particle couldn't possibly exist. When asked about this apparent contradiction and denial of his own research, Doctor Oswald Cropper simply said: "It depends on how you look at things, don't it?"

And the precarious balance of society's values continued its shift. What was up, came down.

Jerry liked visiting his Grandpa Oswald's lab. It smelled musty; the air was filled with the smells of spices and incense. The room was filled with all manner of amazing and wonderful things, powerful things, and things of power (which were not, Grandpa Oswald explained, the same).

The shelves were lined with jars filled with eyes (yes, real eyes, but of what?) and an assortment of snakes and lizards; dried bats hung from the ceiling, intricate containers filled with colored powders lined other shelves, and best of all, along the back wall sat an ancient Chinese apothecary's chest filled with dried potions.

Tapestries picturing beasts that couldn't exist hung on the walls and jade figurines of other creatures lined the windowsill. The sound system played tonal music (composed by his grandmother) that made you feel odd but good.

And when the weather was good, the sun shining, the windows were always open. Birds flocked to the lab, landing on the windowsill, to eat the pieces of cookie Grandpa Oswald put there, and to sing to him, their songs blending strangely with the tonal music.

The only thing even close to being ordinary in the lab, the only thing whose purpose and meaning was obvious, was the sign over his desk. Someone had burned the familiar words into actual wood. Real wood! It had to be worth a fortune.

It said: "A good world requires magical thinking because magic shows us the way to happiness and magic includes science."

Everyone had a version of that motto these days. Jerry knew that the words were Great Granny Jill's, but this sign was hand-crafted by his Grandpa Oswald. It was a proud thing to be the grandson of the first of the great magicians, the master of the Nudge and the Force, the techniques that had paved the way for life as they knew it. But then, Jerry liked the time he spent with his Grandpa Moses too, and the two of them couldn't be more different.

"There is a difference between science and magic," he said. "There is what is proven and reliably demonstrated, and the things that seem to work."

Of course, most people thought Grandpa Moses was strange and out of touch and so, he had never been an important person, like Grandpa Oswald. But Jerry liked the summers he was allowed to spend working in Grandpa Moses' machine shop. He found making precision parts every bit as satisfying as he did when weaving complex spells with Grandpa Oswald and learning to make potions.

Even though everyone wanted you to take sides, to choose between science and magic, Jerry didn't understand why. The world seemed plenty big enough for both of them and he'd learned that you could use one to help the other work even better.

"People seem to have trouble juggling the idea that both can have value," Grandpa Oswald told him.

"Why?" he asked.

"I'm not sure. But at your age, I liked using both, just like you. As I got older, I found that people insisted it was one or the other." His eyes twinkled. "For me, heck, I just found it a lot more fun to use magic, especially since everyone else chose science. It was at the top of the heap. And then my science skills sort of slipped away from me. But you can count on that to change again."

Then, Jerry understood. "What goes up..."

About Ed Teja
A traveling storyteller

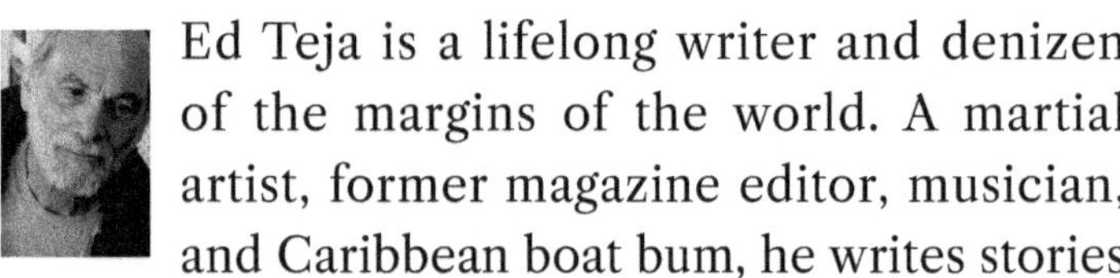Ed Teja is a lifelong writer and denizen of the margins of the world. A martial artist, former magazine editor, musician, and Caribbean boat bum, he writes stories about the people he meets and places he goes — stories that reach deep into the odd corners of the world that often disappear into the margins, and tell of the amazing, often strange, people that inhabit those places.

To stay in touch, learn about new books and special offers, sign up for his newsletter and get a free short story.

Find many more of his books at www.edteja.com

If you enjoyed this story

you might like...

His hands shook slightly, and sweat beaded on his forehead, big drops that threatened to run down into his eyes sooner rather than later. He kept his hands in the air, in plain sight, right about level with his ears.

The curious symmetry of the posture struck him for no apparent reason, none he could think of. He let out a long breath.

"Tell me what you want me to do," he said in his calmest voice.

Steve Mingus stood behind the counter of his store, shaking his head. He'd backed away from the register and had his back against the rack of cigarettes and some odds and ends.

In front of him, on the other side of the counter, stood a young man, dressed in dark jeans with a hole in one knee, and a black hoodie, and his face covered by one of those anonymous hacker masks.

He wore black gloves and was waving a gun, a 9-mm automatic, in Steve's face.

The kid hadn't said a word, just walked into the store and pulled out the damn gun, but he radiated waves of fear and desperation.

The thing to do, Steve told himself, was to stay calm. Calmness never provoked anyone.

Steve glanced down and caught a tantalizing glimpse of the gun they kept behind the counter. The sweet little revolver was easily within his reach. Marjorie, his wife, had insisted they buy the thing and keep it there. She was good with it, better than him, although he'd passed his tests. It had seemed like a good idea, a sensible one... at the time. And she was right about where to put it, too.

Clever, Marjorie was. He could reach it in a single motion.

The problem was he could feel how strung out this kid was... all wired emotionally and maybe on drugs too (he couldn't really tell, not under the circumstances). That made him irrational and unpredictable. Well, robbing a store in broad daylight when there were three CCTV cameras running didn't strike him as exactly rational, but some people seemed to work out a logic that made it make sense.

And the kid had prepared. With the stuff he was wearing, Steve wouldn't be able to tell the cops if he was white, black, or purple, much less start on distinguishing features. He was a featureless kid.

Read the rest at: **https://books2read.com/u/4 NjxOW**